DADDY FORGOT MY DINNER

nuggies™

Story by Jeff Minich

Illustration by Renan Garcia

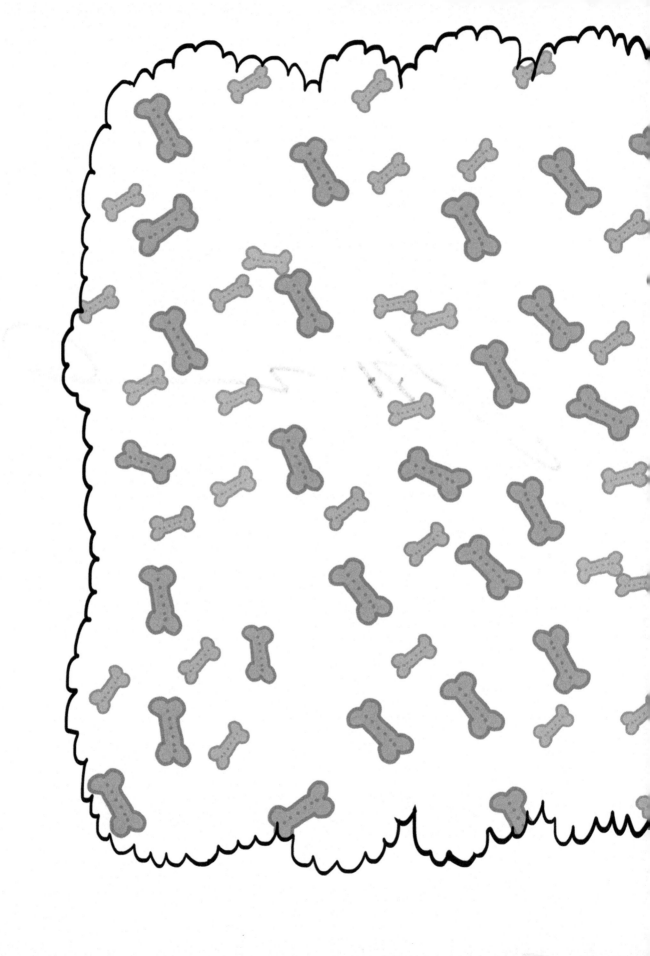

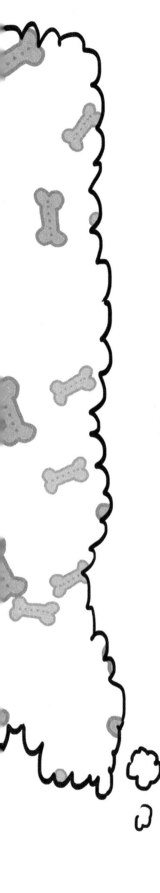

Published in the United States by Nuggies Inc,
Boulder, Colorado 80301

ISBN: 978-0-9862224-3-6

Visit us Online!
www.getnuggies.com

CHOMPER is a very hungry Nuggie. He'll do almost anything for a treat or a bite to eat.

He gets very worried when he's left home all alone with an empty bowl

CHOMPER

But "Trouble" is Chomper's middle name

Eating every thing.
in sight

doesn't seem so
naughty

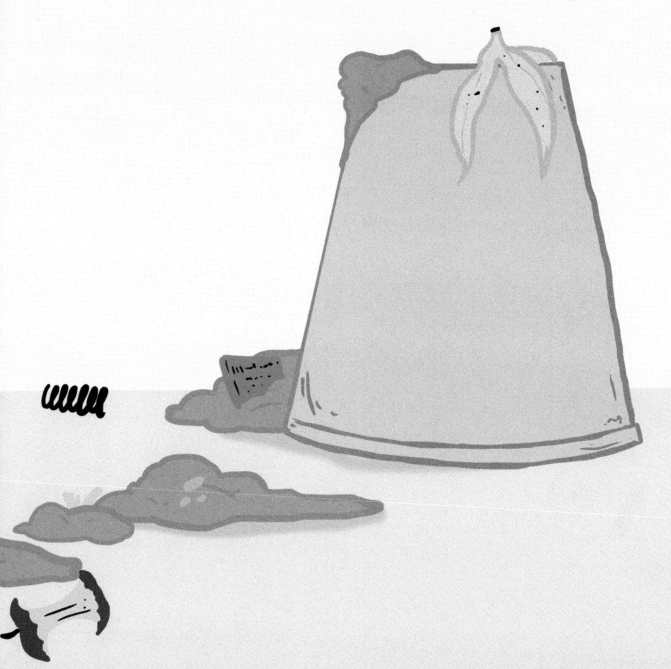

When you're a cute and sweet little Nuggie

Uh Oh! Chomper is awake again with nothing to do ...

So he searches
everywhere to

find some
more food

Round and around he goes

If only he had wings he could fly right up!

There's only one thing to do when you've run out of luck...

Take a nice long nap, please don't interrupt!

Uh Oh ! Still

no dinner!

Chomper will do almost anything to keep fron getting thinner

Sometimes just waiting patiently is the very best way to get what you need

CPSIA information can be obtained
at www.ICGtesting.com
Printed in the USA
LVOW06*0429010217

522838LV00002B/2/P